Sweetheart's Devil

Lexi Gray

Thank you!

Dedication

My lovelies...I know I left you on read last time, but I don't
want to do that...
Don't make me do that again.
XOXO – Lexi

Blurb

Birdie

Time. It's a continuous series of events that occur in succession, from past through the present and to the future. It's something that we can't define unless we can fathom what exactly it is. We don't realize that time is precious...until time no longer exists.

Scout

Who knew life wouldn't be worth fighting if the one person you shared it with was no longer here? Like the wind, she's gone. There's no telling where she went, but one thing I know for sure? I will find her, for she is mine.

Trigger Warnings

Fast burn, open-door sex, historical sexual assault trauma (partially on-screen, no descriptives), character growth, BDSM elements, breeding kink, pregnancy, on-screen torture (not main character).

Author Note

PLEASE DO NOT SKIP

My Dearest Readers,

I want to express that this is not an educational book and not meant to be interpreted as following a specific person's trauma besides Birdie. Everyone who suffers from S/A has different experiences, different healing processes, and different levels of growth from that. Please be kind to one another and myself as this book is not meant to be an actual portrayal of events. It's a work of fiction with **sprinkled** elements of *my* truth.

I appreciate every single person who braves to read this book.

I love you all.

-Lexi Gray

Chapter One

BIRDIE

Pain envelops my being as shivers wrack my body. A cough makes its way up my throat, and as I try to inhale, I immediately taste smoke. Peering through my eyes, it's hard to see through the tears blurring my vision, smoke is billowing from my car.

Confused, I try to sit up, only to realize that I can't move. My head is light, as if all the blood has rushed straight to it. Blinking rapidly to try and clear my sight, there is something yellow dancing around in front of me, but I don't know where it's coming from. I do my best to clear the brain fog and it doesn't take long for me to notice that I'm inside my car. Upside down.

"Shit," I mutter, pressing a hand to my stomach as everything from earlier comes flooding back. The positive test. The photo. Driving like a fucking idiot. Getting smashed into from the side. Then...nothing. "Shit!" I scream, anger flooding my body. Gripping my stomach is almost too much movement as my entire body feels far too heavy, which is most likely from being tipped on my head.

With the blood rush, it's hard to think. My entire body is pressing into the seatbelt, which is the only thing keeping me where I'm at. Moving slowly, I try to take note of any injuries. There is nothing immediately from what I can tell, no cramping or blood.

I look around but I'm limited on what I can see. I hear a vibration and see a cell phone lit up with Sophia calling. If I can just grab it then she can send someone to help. Reaching out, I stretch my arm and get close. Pushing further, I barely get my fingertip on it. I need just another inch and maybe I could reach the answer button. I scoot a little more hoping it will be enough when I hear the crunch of glass.

Stilling, it happens again, this time closer. "Hello?" I call out, praying that it wasn't just a figment of my imagination. No one responds, but the crunching gets closer and closer, louder and louder. "Hello? I need help! I'm stuck in the seatbelt and I can't get undone. Can you call 911? Please?"

The longer the silence stands, the more terrified I feel. "Hello! I'm here. Help me, please!" I scream as loud as I can, but it's like I'm unheard.

Terror and unease fill me rapidly as I desperately keep trying to grab the phone then suddenly a man's hand reaches in and snatches it. I can't see him, but his deep voice sends chills through my spine.

"Yes, sir. She is trapped in the car as agreed upon. My job is done. I have her cell phone. I will dispose of it as I leave the site."

Who is this? Why is this happening to me? What does he mean the job is done? What job?

"Please," I whimper as the blood in my head finally manages to catch up to me. My vision begins to darken and the last thing I think of before I black out is, I hope my baby survives this.

Chapter Two

ᛟ SCOUT ᛟ

My fist collides with his face, his entire body jerking to the left with the impact. He can't go anywhere due to the ropes holding him in place, yet I hold no mercy. The things he did to her are unforgivable and will not go unpunished. Birdie may feel like she let it go, may have been able to heal from those wounds, but the pain he caused her? She will never be able to forget that. So, I will make him suffer for every day she doubted herself, for every nightmare, and for taking something from her that wasn't his to take. . Then after? He will never see the light of day again.

"You're fucking worthless," I spit, watching the wad of saliva land on his nose. The whole top of his head is red and blistered from the flames, oozing blood like rivers down the side of his head. .

"No," he mutters, his body shaking with the effort he has had to take to hold himself steady. I will give him a bit of credit. Having burned his lashes, brows, and all of his hair off, he is holding steadfast. Woefully for him, that won't be lasting much longer.

"Get him up," I bark, watching as Massimo's men start moving immediately. The fucker tries fighting them the best he can, but he is up against several hard trained men. Yanking on his arms, they manage to get his arms in front of him and into the slip knot quickly. His arms jerk above his body and he is forced to either hang by his shoulder sockets or stand on his tiptoes. Neither are long-lasting options. I wait until the men step away from him, letting him struggle to grip the ground and stop swinging.

Once I'm fully satisfied with how he is presented, I mosey over to the table of devices.

"I don't think you need us," Massimo calls jokingly, a few of the others snicker along with him.

"You're correct, but it doesn't hurt to have a bit of an audience. I love humiliating others," I say, glancing over my shoulder at him. Garrett Weller, the man who touched someone who isn't his. He took something valuable. While I know I can't get it back, I can absolutely redeem the cost of it.

Garrett seems to stumble in the short span, struggling to remain in one spot. Lucky for me, I'm going to make his life miserable. Unlucky for him, he may tear both shoulders clean from their sockets.

My fist tightens around the end of a baseball bat, I lift to test the weight in my hands. I relax my wrist and let it swing a bit, determining the type of control I will have on it. It's either this or a collapsible baton.

The bat is going to hurt a fuck ton more.

My choice is made.

"Heads or tails?" I call out, smacking the bat in my other hand as I stroll back over to him.

"Do I need to get a coin?" Massimo questions, his arms crossed over his chest and leaning against the wall.

"Someone answer the damn question," I sigh as I let the bat drop to bounce off the toe of my boot.

"Tails!"

"Finally." Smiling at him, I rear the bat back and let it fly. His scream curdles through the small area as the swing makes contact with his tail bone. The crunch of bone soothes the rage burning inside of me, if only for a few seconds. He didn't understand what I meant when I said I would make him wish he wasn't born.

"No, no," he begs, snot sliding down his face pathetically. "I don't even know her, I swear." He continues to sob as his legs finally give out from under him. The sharp snap of his shoulders removing themselves from their sockets makes him scream some more. Walking to the front of his body, I swing the bat toward his groin, stopping mere centimeters away from him. The flinch of his reaction has his body jerking backward and grinding his already broken bones.

"Fuck," Massimo groans from behind me. Looking over my shoulder, his fingers are flying over the screen on his phone. "The girls are blowing up my phone." Furrowing my brows, I let the bat drop with a clatter onto the floor and pull my own out. Sure enough, there are several missed calls from Birdie, Sofia, Vivianna, and a slew of unknown numbers. I immediately try to dial Birdie back but it goes straight to voicemail.

"Call Sofia," I demand, redialing Birdie incessantly.

Scrolling through the onslaught of messages, my heart gets faster and faster, and I'm sure I look as though I have seen a ghost.

Sofia:

> How could you? She trusted you, ya know.

> I hope this is one giant misunderstanding.

> Call me ASAP.

> Fuck, call me back!

> Birdie took off, we tried to stop her.

Viv:

> You're a fucking scum bag.

> You know what? I'm giving you the benefit of the doubt.

> None of you will call us back? Boning one another or something?

> Birdie just peeled out of the vineyard. Call one of us back.

> It's been an hour and she's not back. WTF?

"Fuck, fuck, fuck," I chant. Scrolling further along, I whip my head up to look at Massimo. He looks almost as panicked as me.

"Take him down and chain him to the wall. We will be back later," Massimo commands. They quickly follow their marching orders, throwing Garrett around to get him down. Massimo and I don't wait around to make sure they get their shit done. Tossing the keys to his driver, we jump into the car and peel out of the drive.

Chapter Three

SCOUT

"Take a breather," Viv says, putting her hand in front of my face and stopping me from physically raging. I have no other choice but to relax. I will not take my anger out on these ladies. It's not their fault. Hell, it's not even mine. I fully blame the idiot women who decided it was a great idea to assault me then spread it around like a fucking gossip magazine.

Taking several deep breaths, it doesn't necessarily help calm me, but it gives me a moment to just focus on my next steps.

"That was your car, right?" Massimo asks, bringing Sofia in close. She whispers something in his ear, too low for any of us to hear. He blanches, his head swinging to look down at her before whipping to look at me.

"Uhm, yeah?" I question as he leans down into her ear and she nods vigorously. His soft curse has everyone straightening their spines. "I have a tracker on the car. I should be able to locate it." Closing out of the other apps, I quickly pull open the AllTrack app that one of my buddies installed for me a while back. Refreshing several times, it takes nearly ten minutes in complete silence before the flashing blue dot pops up.

"Got it!" I announce, just about ready to shout in joy. I hold my excitement inside because I have no idea what we will find.

"Ladies, hang back for now," Massimo adds, dropping a kiss to Sofia's head before stepping back.

"What? No!"

"Absolutely not!"

"She could be hurt!"

The three ladies bombard us with complaints, defiantly disagreeing with his order. He sighs, glancing toward me for help.

"If she is hurt, what are you going to do?" I ask, stopping them in their complaints. "Can any of you provide lifesaving measures? Do a tourniquet with a belt? What if someone is waiting for us there? You all could be bait and we'd never know because we're flying blind."

"But if she is hurt, she will want-"

"If she is hurt, we will need to figure out how to help her. Too many people can create an overwhelming situation. Honestly, it can make the situation worse than it already is. Do you want to frighten her more than she might already be?" They mumble to themselves, not replying to my questions but also not protesting anymore. "We need to be able to protect her and ourselves without putting your lives at risk." The girls finally seem to digress as they sit at the counter of the bar. Unlocking my phone, I note that the dot hasn't moved at all.

"We need to go," I call, ready to run out of the place and start on foot to her. Massimo kisses Sofia's hair and peels himself away from her.

Loading back into the SUV, the driver takes off toward where I pulled her location. It says it's a thirty-minute drive, but with the way he is driving, it should only take about twenty.

"Sof said something interesting," Massimo starts, looking up from his phone. He opens his mouth a few times before closing it, obviously struggling with what he is trying to say.

"Spit it out," I demand softly. He swallows thickly and looks as though he regrets saying anything to begin with.

"The girls think Birdie is pregnant."

Time seems to slow even more after that simple word. Ringing takes over my ears as I struggle to wrap my head around it.

Pregnant.

"What?" I whisper and squint to watch his lips.

"Pregnant." I don't hear him say it with the pressure building in my head, but it's clear that's the word he is forming on his lips. Words don't come to me at that moment. I'm struck in literal silence, unable to wrap my mind around it.

"How?" I mutter. Leaning forward, I drop my head into my hands and try to calculate everything in my head. It's a rhetorical question which he knows, so he lets me sit with the thoughts whirling in my brain. "Shit." I mean, we were sort of leaving it up to fate, really. If it happened, great. If not, we could always keep trying.

That would explain the extreme reaction, though. She is already not feeling like herself then add the shitty photo she must have gotten...that's a rotten fucking equation. My phone is proof that she tried to call me. *She tried*. Now we're adding fuel to the fire with her stranded in fuck knows where.

"Hey." A hand lands swiftly on my shoulder shaking me out of my darkening thoughts. "Don't beat yourself up over this. There was nothing you could have done to prevent this."

"I could have answered my phone," I croak through the thick lump sitting in my throat. "There is so much I could have done to prevent this."

"It's the past. Is there anything we can do about it?" Shaking my head, I pinch my eyes closed harder to get the images of what I could possibly be going into out of my head. "We need to prepare for the worst case scenario, man."

"How far are we?" I ask. Sitting up, I lean my head back on the head rest and close my eyes.

"Five minutes, sirs," the driver calls from the front. The only acknowledgment I give is a silent nod. I can't tell if it's the anticipation of seeing Birdie possibly mangled all to pieces or what, but my heart sits directly in my throat as we drive in complete silence. My brain comes to several different conclusions.

She is wrapped around a tree somewhere in a ravine. The car is wrapped around a tree, pierced through it, and she is stuck inside. There is a possibility that the car is flipped over and a tree is stuck through the middle of it, the metal grinding could probably scare—

"We're here, I believe," the driver calls back. I yank the car door open, hopping out and looking around for her or the car. It doesn't take long for me to notice red and yellow flames pillowing from between the trees. I take off towards it.

"Scout, wait!" Someone screams after me. I refuse to listen. Birdie is in there. I slide down the side of the hill, trying and failing, to stay upright. My foot catches on a protruding root and I tumble. I land harshly right in front of the smoking vehicle.

"Birdie!" I shout, standing on shaky legs and looking inside the broken windows. Strands of blonde hair sit on the shards of glass on the other side, but at least I can see her..

"Scout," she mumbles, her voice hoarse and scratchy, most likely from breathing in the smoke.

"I'm here, baby," I coo, brushing my hand over her hair and pressing my palm into the cut on her head to stop the bleeding. She groans against the pressure and raises a hand to push me away, yet it falls back down after only being raised a few inches.

The cocking of a gun echoes behind me before something is shoved into the back of my head. I freeze.

"Now, now, pretty boy," a guy taunts, shoving me forward into the upturned car. My stomach sinks more as the smoke in the hood starts billowing faster and thicker. "You touched mine; I touch yours."

"What are you talking about?" I ask calmly, not wanting to raise his hackles any further. He and I are both already on edge, there is no doubt he would pull the trigger at the slightest move. That doesn't mean I'm just going to take it lying down. Gun shots ring out from above us, and the guy behind me laughs.

"Sounds like they are getting taken care of. Maybe you'll think not to touch something that doesn't belong to you."

"I have no clue what you're even talking about," I retort, trying to wrack my brain with clues. Nothing comes up, and I'm left frozen with Birdie trapped in a car that looks about ready to combust.

"You're part of *his* crew. If he didn't fuck us over, I wouldn't be here enacting revenge." His tone gets colder by the second, though he must realize my continued confusion with my silence. "What about you kissing my wife?" He shouts as he slams the butt of the gun against my head. Hissing with pain, I quickly shove my hand into my waistband and pull out my own gun. Pointing it directly at him, we remain at a standoff. His face is visibly red, his hand shaking. His head is muddied, which I can use to my advantage.

"*She* kissed *me!* I didn't want her then and I certainly don't want her now!" I shout in defense, still attempting to get everything else he said to comprehend. "I'm not a part of anyone's crew. I'm just a fighter!" That part may be a small lie, but it's not far from the truth. I do fight, it just usually ends with my anger faded and another demon sent back to hell.

"I should have fucking killed you that night, but she begged me not to." His laugh is cold blooded. The second he drops his head back in a mocking laugh, I smash my finger on the trigger. The gunpowder ignites as the hammer strikes the primer in the gun. The ricochet echoes through the trees, and he stumbles backward in shock, almost as if he couldn't believe I would actually do it. His hand drops to his wound where blood is pouring out of him. Face dropping in shock, I watch as his brain processes what happened. I'm immediately off the ground and running toward him.

My brain is hazy, my vision blurry from the lack of adjustment from being hit in the head to standing. Grabbing his gun, I rip it away from him and stare down for a moment. I try, and fail, to place him in my brain. He is not familiar, but I know who he meant when he talked about the kiss.

I don't have time to dwell on it right now. Shoving both guns into my waist, I level back down with Birdie to see her eyes closed. Loud chatter comes down the hill as the gun shots quiet down. Looking up, several men come storming down toward us, and I'm able to quickly recognize them as Massimo's men.

Two others go around to the passenger side and start blasting it with foam from an extinguisher. Massimo meets me at her side of the car, and together we rip the door open with adrenaline force. She stays pinned to the seat by her belt as welts have already embedded themselves into her and are seeping blood. Grabbing a knife, I quickly cut through the seat belt. With a snap, her small body tumbles from the vehicle, blood pouring from her head and lower body.

"I called medical, it will take them too long to get here. We need to get her to the hospital," Massimo says, bringing the phone back to his ear. Checking her fingers and toes, she moves and flinches after being poked, so I can only pray that she doesn't have a neck injury.

Hoisting her bridal style into my arms, I trek out of the ravine as gently and quickly as possible. She moans and groans as we go, complaining quietly of pain in her stomach and shoulder. I don't give myself time to focus on the potential of her stomach pain.

"It's going to be alright, baby bird," I murmur softly into her hair, pressing my toe on a root to ensure it's stable. Once I'm sure it's not going to give way, I push our weight up on it and keep climbing. Massimo and the driver hustle up to the top and yell at one another to get the vehicle flipped around.

"He is going to take photos. We'll figure out who did this," Massimo assures as I get to the top. Another guy from his car steps out and begins taking a bunch of pictures of the car. I want to ask him about the man, who he is and what he was talking about, but Birdie is my priority right now, and I can't afford to lose her.

Thankfully they were able to put out the flames before it could explode. He opens the door and helps me situate Birdie into the backseat. I hoist myself up onto the seat next to her and place her head in my lap. Her eyes are closed, her face almost peaceful despite the blood coating her face.

"Scout," she croaks again, her hands shaking in an effort to reach up to me. I grasp her bloody hand in mine, twining our fingers together. "I'm sorry."

"Shh," I hush, rubbing my thumb over her cheek bone while I keep pressure on her head. "You have nothing to be sorry about."

"The baby," she chokes, blood sitting on her teeth as she coughs harshly. It's wet and unsavory, making me wince for her pain.

"It's okay, my love. It will be okay."

Chapter Four

BIRDIE

My body is on fire. I'm not sure how, but I can feel it. It's like my bones are submerged in lava and simmering on low until they finally boil over. At this point, I think they are waiting for the explosion.

Beep.

"...not good."

Beep.

"You're sure..."

Beep.

Each voice is muted. I can hear them. I hear several people talking around me, though I *can't* hear. It's like a river rushing through my ears or waves crashing nonstop against the shoreline. It's impossible to make out full sentences, yet they are *here*. The more important question is: who are *they*? A sharp trilling *beep* is the only clear thing I can make out. It's annoying. If I could, I would topple the damn thing over just to shut it up.

I do my best to open my eyes, let them know the amount of immense pain that I'm in, but they refuse to do anything besides remain closed. From inside of my body, it feels as though I'm wiggling around and making my fingers twitch. From their continued conversation, they either don't see it or I'm not actually moving anything.

"...clavicle grade three separat..." Irritation blossoms in me as they speak as though I'm not here.

Groaning internally, I finally manage to grip the sheets under my fingers and squeeze. The change in feeling is the only indicator that I actually did it. Bubbles form in my throat, liquid seemingly coming up my neck and into my mouth.

I inhale, only to realize that I can't. Eyes flying open, bright light immediately blinding me as I fight my limbs to move. No noise comes from me, my hands barely raising from the bed while I choke. I see people in the room, I don't know who they are, but they are not paying attention to me at all. Their arms are raised, waving around while I wish they would look back at me. Finally, one of them looks over their shoulder to see me struggling. He doesn't waste any time in running out to the hall. No noise passes through the overbearing *whooshing* in my ears, yet when nurses flood the room and kick the rest of the people out.

Heat breaks over my face, my brain turns foggy. I can barely feel the prodding of hands along my body as I fight to breathe.

Chapter Five

SCOUT

I rub my thumb over Birdie's pale hand. Her fingers lay limp around mine as I grip hers for dear life. If I hold on just a bit tighter, it might make her realize there is someone here for her. Grounding her. Protecting her. It's been a living, breathing hell since we brought her in. They wouldn't let me back with her until they got her in the ICU and stable. Even then it was a struggle. Finally, Massimo ended up pulling his weight to get them to let me in.

Birdie and I are practically fucking married...just without the wedding or the proposal.

"Well, shit," I mutter to myself, dropping my sight to her slender fingers. It would be easy to slip a ring onto her digit and she would be none the wiser. When she wakes up, she would get a happy shock.

There would be no asking though. She *will* be my wife. End of story.

Before I can think anymore into it, the nurse strolls in with the little notepad in hand checking over Birdie like she is made of glass. I suppose that is the case since she has been lying motionless in the bed for several days. If she were awake, I just know she would throw a fit about being tended to. She has always been a bit of a stubborn woman.

"Her signs are stable, but I'm afraid some of the testing is not good," she sighs as she jots down things from the monitor onto the pad.

"What do you mean?" Brows furrowing, I grip Birdie's hand tightly in mine. The nurse raises her own skeptical eyebrow, glancing to where my fingers are interlocked with Birdie's lax ones. The nurse sighs heavily, her gaze flitting to the door for a moment.

"I'm not supposed to tell you this…"

"Please?" I beg, unable to handle any more waiting. Questions have gone unanswered for the entirety of Birdie's stay, and I'm quite honestly ready to jump out of my seat to start demanding some damn answers.

"The baby…" she mutters, grabbing a syringe out of her pocket and twisting it onto the line. "Is fine. Doc wasn't sure if you had known…"

"You're sure?" The air stays caught in my lungs while I wait for her final acknowledgement. "How could they not know that I know? I have been begging them to tell me for the last four days!"

"Keep your voice down," she scolds, untwisting and disposing of the line. "The doctor will be in shortly." With that, she turns on her heel and hustles out of the room. I don't want to rat her out to anyone, but I can't help the tears of joy filling my eyes.

It takes a moment to digest that the tests *aren't* good. I jump out of my chair, only for the doc to open the door and greet me happily.

"How are you hanging in there, son?" He asks, giving my hand a bone crushing shake. I squeeze just as aggressively, which only makes him smile wider.

"I'm alright, doc. Just waiting for her to wake up, ya know?" Even I can hear the partial hopelessness in my voice, the anguish I feel finally starting to leak from me. There is only so much I can take from not being able to hear her voice, see her beautiful brown eyes...

"It may be a little while. After conducting a neuroradiology, it appears Ms. Yarrow suffers from a Traumatic Brain Injury, or TBI. We anticipate that she will remain unconscious for quite some time, which is encouraged to give her brain and body some respite."

"So, it could be longer?" I ask dejectedly. She needs to heal from the shit she has gone through, but I just want her to wake up. I just want to know she is going to be okay.

"Potentially, yes. She also has a clavicle grade III separation. We are going to refer her to physical therapy while she is admitted to assist in the healing process, but she may need surgery in the future. With her current...condition," he pauses, glancing away from me for a moment to the passed-out female. I follow his gaze, watching her chest move up and down evenly. The tube in her throat surely helps with that.

"She is pregnant, isn't she?" I whisper, knowing full well that she is carrying our baby. The nurse blabbed, but that doesn't mean I can't have the doctor confirm it also. My cheeks burn from the smile I'm sporting knowing that my beautiful girl is alive, then add a baby on top of that...

"She is," he confirms. I want to shout from the rooftops, call out to the world that she is officially mine in every possible way. "But as I was saying about her shoulder, it cannot be repaired at this moment. I can say with certainty that she will need surgery in the next couple of years."

"What does the recovery look like?" I ask, glancing over to him again. He opens his mouth to answer when a rasping gasp draws our attention. Rushing over, I place my hands on her face and watch her pupils quickly dilate. From the small amounts of medical knowledge I know, that's not a good sign.

"Birdie," I call, gently patting her face.

"Move out of the way!" The doctor shouts as he shoves me away from her. She struggles to breathe even more when an awful, dreadful ring echoes from somewhere in the room.

"Shit, code blue!" He shouts and starts grabbing at things in the room. The nurses flood the room, "get the crash cart!"

Slowly I'm swept from the room and into the hallway once more. Like worker bees, they fly in and out of the room as they work to stabilize her. Her heart may have stopped, but mine won't stop soaring far too quickly. My knees no longer have the ability to hold me up, and I go crumbling to the floor in agony.

I celebrated far too soon.

A hand lands on my shoulder and my instincts kick in. Grabbing their wrist, I lift my elbow and twist downward. The person comes stumbling in front of me, landing on their knees next to me.

"Fuck!" I bark, scooting away from Massimo while he rubs his shoulder with a smirk on his face. "I'm sorry, man, I just-"

"It was my fault for coming up on you," he cuts me off, his hand held up in the universal stop sign. "I didn't realize you had mastered the art of jiu jitsu."

"I haven't. I mastered the art of 'I seem to work with the mafia and I want to keep myself safe.' Ya know?"

"That's why you carry a gun," he says as if it's the most obvious thing in the world. For him, he may be able to walk around with that thing wherever he wants to go, but I can't.

"Yeah, well, it must be nice to have privileges," I scoff, sliding down ever further and landing on my ass.

"It's not a privilege. When you start from nothing, you can make yourself into something. It's fear, not privilege."

"I'm sorry," I sigh again, bringing my knees in front of me and dropping my head onto them. My brain is far too full for everything else at this point.

"Believe me, I know what it's like to be on the brink of losing someone so important." He slides down the wall next to me, laying his arms over his knees.

"You look ridiculous," I laugh sadly. He is in a suit, the normal attire for the royalty himself, and he is sitting on the floor with me.

"I'm sure I do, but you do too." He bumps his shoulder with me, and in that moment, I realize that everything is going to be okay. I have hope that Birdie is going to be just fine.

Chapter Six

FLASHBACK - FOUR YEARS AGO

BIRDIE

"*I fucking hate this song,*" *I grumble as I click the next button on my iPod. Scout uploaded* I Wanna Love You *by Akon that he's had on repeat for the past year, and I've seriously had enough of it. I'll admit that it's super catchy, but now that it's been playing non-stop every day on the radio before school, I just want to make it stop.*

"Hey, baby," Scout purrs jokingly, sliding up next to me on my walk. He slings his arm over my shoulder and drops a kiss on my hair. Giggling, I shove him away playfully.

"Hey yourself, I can't believe I let you burn me a playlist," I say, feigning irritation. The look on his face is pure stricken horror.

"Are you saying my taste in music is garbage?" He brings his hand to his chest, inhaling deeply dramatically. Rolling my eyes, I take the headphones off and put them on his head. Ms. New Booty *by Bubba Sparxxx blasts so loud even I can*

hear it. He grimaces and takes them off with a slight tint on his cheeks.

"So?" I sass, my hands landing on my hips as I stop to assess him. He shoves his hands in his pockets, his chin dipped down to his chest.

"Yeah, that was not a great choice." He shrugs, glancing at my current outfit. I'm wearing my new pleated skirt with tights underneath, my new cut off striped tee-shirt and my converse. I got four compliments on the outfit just today! "I can admit that wasn't the best song choice."

Jaw dropping, I smack my hand on his forehead. "You don't feel warm," I mumble, narrowing my eyes at him. "Are you feeling okay?" He swats my hand away from him, lacing our fingers together with a laugh.

"Hey now, I can admit when I'm wrong," he shrugs. He brings my hand to his mouth and places a gentle kiss on the back of it. It's my turn for my cheeks to turn warm. "I'm meeting a buddy later tonight to hit the town. You should come."

"I don't know, I have to study for a mid-term coming up." I know I should say no out-right. Professor Zig hates me to his core and will fail me with every chance he can get. But Scout juts his bottom lip out and gives me these puppy eyes that I can never resist.

"Fine," I sigh exasperatedly. "I'm only staying for an hour, then I have to go," I laugh, jerking him along with me as we walk back to the carpark.

"How is she doing, doc?" His voice sounds familiar, but I can't place it. "It's been several days without any update or anything."

"She doesn't have..." the man's voice fades out, who I assume is the doctor, and I can't hear anything besides bitter mumbling between the two deep voices.

I can hear them...only it doesn't sound like them anymore...

"I think I'm going to head out," I call over the booming speakers. Scout laughs with his friend who has a girl sidled up next to both of them. He gives me a thumbs up, though I don't know if he even heard me. I motioned over my shoulder with my thumb, and he waves me off. Okay, so he did hear me

.

I figured he would at least walk me out to an Uber, yet he seems so enraptured by the two girls and his friend that I'm just a post-thought. I'm not going to complain. It was nice of him to even invite me out. I just stayed at the counter and to myself all night anyway, so my leaving isn't going to bother him any.

Pulling up the app, there are several listings but they're all booked for at least two hours. Looking around, the streets seem packed enough for me to walk to the bus stop. I should be able to get back to town from there. In this moment, I'm thankful I wore my sneakers.

Several groups bypass me going toward the clubs as I leave. Gaggling girls, frat boys on the hunt, everyone in between. My phone buzzes in my purse, and I pull it out to see that there is a text notification. My heart skips a beat for a second thinking it was Scout. Unlocking the device, my hopes are immediately crushed. It was from Scout, but not how I envisioned it.

Scout:

> **Hey, don't wait up. We're going bar hopping with the girls. Not sure when I'll be home *smiley emoji***

Huffing a frustrated laugh, I lock the phone and walk faster to the stop. The farther I get, the quieter the streets become. As I approach the empty lot, the silence is loud. Looking at the street, a set of tail lights flash orange, and I groan in annoyance. If that was the last bus, so help me...

Opening the app, I check the time and stop location.

"Are you fucking kidding me?" I groan, dropping heavily into the seat.

"Did I miss it?" A guy shouts, running toward me. Furrowing my brows, I sink lower into the seat to make myself a smaller target. "Shit," he groans, his hands gripping his hair in visible frustration. He drops next to me on the bench and sighs heavily. After a minute, he glances toward me with a small smile. Something in it immediately sends chills down my body. Giving him a tight lipped smile of my own, I scoot farther down the bench.

"I'm Garrett," he says, reaching his hand out toward me. "I figured if we're going to be camping on this bench, we may as well make acquaintances."

"Uhm," I hesitate, looking from his hand to his face. He doesn't waiver, keeping it stretched far longer than socially normal. "Raven," I reply though I don't return the handshake. I refuse to give any potential identifiers to find me later.

"Raven," he purrs as he moves a bit closer to me. "A pretty girl like you shouldn't be out this late. There are monsters out here in the dark."

"I can handle myself, thanks," I scoff, standing from the bench and backing up. "Nice to meet you, though I am meeting a friend later and need to figure out how to get there."

"You're not meeting a friend," he retorts sarcastically, grabbing my wrist and pulling my body to his.

"Let go of me," I snap. Struggling in his hold, he keeps me tightly tucked into him. "Get your hands off-" his spare hand

lands harshly on my cheek, my head whipping to the side as copper fills my mouth.

"You're going to shut your fucking mouth," he grunts, moving us backward. I continue struggling against his hold, unsure what will happen if I don't fight back.

"Fuck you!" I spit, literally landing a wad of saliva in his eye. His grip loosens enough for me to get his grip off of me. Taking off in the opposite direction, I scream.

"Help me!" I don't want to risk glancing behind me, simply running toward where I came from. "Someone please help me!" Those words seem like jamais vu as they leave my mouth, but I don't have the space or brain capacity to think about it too long.

"No one can hear you!" He shouts from behind me, the smacking of his shoes on the concrete growing closer and closer. "You're going to fucking regret running!"

The sidewalk seems to come to an end, a giant brick building taking up my space. What the fuck? Turning left is the only way I can go, so I do. Pity me because it's a fucking dead end.

"No," I gasp, my lungs punching in my gut to catch air while simultaneously refusing to send the oxygen to my brain. Before I can come up with a plan, I'm slammed into the wall roughly.

"You're such a naughty girl," he grunts, moving my hair aside and gripping my neck tightly. Harsh bricks scrape into my cheek, the tip of my nose barely touches the rough wall.

His one hand holds both of mine hostage, not letting up even while I struggle to regain control over myself.

□"Get off me," I squeak through the pressure. A whimper makes its way through my tightly clenched throat. His breath is rancid against my face, almost like his mouth is rotting.

□"You were wearing this short, short scrap of material. Weren't you just asking for it?" His free hand, the one that seems to have a mind of its own, roams my body freely.

□"I didn't wear this for anyone!" I sneer, bringing my knee into his groin. He doubles over, and I manage to slip past him. Just as I take a few steps, my hair is yanked backward. He doesn't waste any time in slamming me into the putrid, damp alley floor.

□"Going to finally take what's mine," he growls in my ear. Snapping my eyes shut, I just will him to leave me alone.

Chapter Seven

SCOUT

It's been three days since they had to sedate her again. I can't even keep track of how long she has been here. My heart hurts just thinking about her pain and discomfort. The doctor's warned me that they weaned her off the medication, but it's up to her on how long it will take for her to come back to me.

Clasping her hand tighter in mine, I kiss her knuckles gently. "If you can hear me, give me a sign that you're going to be okay, baby bird." I sigh against her skin, my eyes squeezed tight in an effort not to cry for the millionth time today.

□"Fuck off." Snapping myself straight, Birdie's eyes are closed but her brows are furrowed. I shoot out of my seat and turn the illumination down for the overhead lights. They are blinding and can give you a headache within minutes of being on. Rushing back to the chair beside her, she is immediately glaring down at me. I can't help but be grateful that she is awake at all. There is fire inside of her. Raw and pure, a flame that I'm willing to burn in as long as she is willing to let me.

"Baby bird," I gasp, a sob suddenly catching in my throat. I didn't think I had anymore tears left to cry, but here I am. A fucking wimp. "I'm so sorry, baby bird."

"The baby?" She asks, shooting upright in the bed. She suddenly looks green, her upper body suddenly off its axis as I catch her sideways fall.

"You can't make any sudden movements. You just..." I pause, staring right into her soul. She is angry. Pissed, actually. But there is also an unrelenting love. That's something I can hold onto while she works her frustrations out on me.

"The. Baby?" She punctuates roughly, weakly pushing me off of her. I let her go, though I stay close enough to keep her hand wrapped in mine. Either she doesn't notice or doesn't care.

"Baby is fine, she is healthy and perfect so far."

"She?" Birdie asks with wonder, her brows creasing in confusion.

"It's too early to tell, but I have a feeling it'll be a little girl." Birdie's eyes immediately soften, and she squeezes back.

"You have a fuck ton of explaining to do," she says, her eyes narrowing at me in a threatening manner. Well, I assume she is trying to be threatening. All I see is a beautiful woman who appears tired, worn out, and emotionally drained. She is nothing less than perfect.

□"I promise I will explain everything once we get you home," I reassure, kissing the back of her knuckles one more time. She nods, looking away from me again and staring off at the other wall. I watch it with her for a few moments, not sure what we're looking at exactly. "What's wrong? I should have called the doctor earlier." Rising from the seat, I don't even take a step away from her before I'm yanked back onto the bed.

□"Make love to me, Scout," she says. It's a quiet and gentle demand, one that wouldn't hold power over anyone who isn't madly in love with her. For her, she holds far more power over me than she realizes.

□"Birdie, you just woke up," I start attempting to reason with her, but her head shakes rapidly from side to side.

□"I just...I need you to erase it again," she whispers as she wraps an arm around my neck to pull me down to her level. I brace my arms on the bed to try and hold on, actively avoiding her hurt shoulder.

□"Wait baby, you were hurt pretty badly in the accident. I don't want to hurt you anymore," I say, shaking my head and I kick myself in the ass. I have never denied her anything she wants. This is definitely a first, and my heart hurts just thinking that I can't give that to her right now.

□"I'm hurting more in here," she pauses and uses her braced arm to point to her head. "I saw things I didn't want to see. Relived them...please help me quiet my thoughts for a while, Scout?"

▢"Baby bird, I'm really trying here." The lump in my throat is large, far too big for me to swallow yet that doesn't stop me from trying. "You're not in the right headspace..."

"Do you love me or not?" She quips, jerking backward to get a better look at me. "Because right now, I'm in a head space where I feel completely alone. It's not going to fucking kill you to kiss me, unless you've thought about breaking up with-"

My lips land on hers heavily, no warning whatsoever. I refuse to have her question my love for her because some fucking whore decided she didn't want to play princess with her boyfriend. Birdie is one of the few individuals I will not risk losing. If she wants me to make her demons go away, then fuck it. Do I feel like it's going to bite me in the ass later? Yes. Will I have her question our every interaction because I won't make love to her? Absolutely not.

So, I have no other choice except to give her what she wants. Not that I'm complaining, I just don't want to hurt her anymore than she already is.

Yanking back, I level her with a gentle but stern gaze. "Last chance. I know you're upset with me, but if I make love to you, right here, right now, there's no running from me." She nods, her arm gripping the nape of my neck with her nails and attempting to claw me back to her. "I love you more than life itself, Birdie. I would give my last breath to you if it meant you could have one more, but you don't get to run. You stay. We talk. We do this. Together. I will beg for the rest of my life for your forgiveness, but you will not retreat into yourself."

"Scout," she starts, but I land my lips right back onto hers cutting her off.

"I'm serious. You need to promise me." Her once hard and brittle gaze softens more and more as we stare through one another. "I can't make love to someone who won't vow to love me back."

"Oh, Scout," she sighs, her hand coming to rest on my cheek. Instinctively I lean into the simple touch. "I promise."

That's all I need to hear. Dipping back down, I kiss her, this time slower and with ease. I pour my heart into this kiss with her, not giving her any reason to doubt my love for her. It may be stupid that I have her promise me something like not running away, but I refuse to have her run into herself. No retreating. It's now or never. Especially after that fucked up photo, I want to do everything in my power to make sure she knows she is loved. I just also don't want to jeopardize her mental health. It's a sticky area, but I'm willing to navigate it for her.

"I love you, baby bird," I whisper against her lips as I dip my tongue to graze her lower lip. Jaw dropping just a hair, I kiss her fervently. She clings to me as if her life depends on it. Clawing her nails deeper into my neck, her grip nearly brings my full body weight onto her. "I don't want to hurt you."

"Scout," she huffs as she begins to retreat. I grab the remote for the hospital bed and lower it more. It can't be flat because of her shoulder and that's perfectly okay with me. Grabbing the edge of the blanket, I yank it off of her which leaves her legs open to my feasting eyes. Even after being in the hospital for multiple days, she is still utter perfection.

I move away from her much to her dismay and scoot further down. She must realize my intentions because she props her knees up and lets them fall out to give me room to work. A low rumble grows inside my chest, her sweet pussy on display for me as I inspect her. She blushes deeply, which most likely is because she is not shaved. Good thing for her, I don't give a fuck. What's that saying? Explore the wilderness.

Just as she goes to shut her thighs, I push them open and spread them with my shoulders as I dive in. One long lick is enough for the little thread of self-restraint to snap. Her good hand slides quickly into my hair as I devour her thoroughly. The noises she makes vary as I go, and when I notice she is getting close to release, I stop. Wave after wave of near orgasmic bliss, I ease her off the ledge.

"Knock it off," she growls, irritation fully engulfing her tone. I chuckle against her, the vibrations causing goosebumps to rise on her flesh under my hands.

"I think you're mistaken, sweetheart," I mumble against her clit, swirling my tongue around it slowly. "This is me groveling. I will eat your pussy for breakfast, lunch, and dinner. I will beg you for forgiveness every single day of my life for something that I didn't even do. That's how much I fucking love you," I pause to bring my fingers to her hole. Inserting a finger slowly, her tight cunt squeezes around me. "But I'm in charge."

Not giving her any more chances to chat, I dive right back in. Shoving my middle finger in with my ring finger and angling them just right, I find her g-spot almost immediately. Her hips buck off the table, her moans echoing off the walls. There is no possibility that someone hasn't heard us, but I don't make that fact known nor do I really care. She is mine to have and to fucking hold, I will do what I damn well please.

If she demands I make her cum, that's what I will fucking do or die trying. Unfortunately for her, that doesn't have to mean I do it right away.

"If I had two fucking arms, I would kill you," she shrieks loudly as I rip away from her right as she was about to cum.

Smirking, I sit up and unbutton my jeans. My cock is already hard from devouring her, so pulling it out is a bit harder without fully standing up. I give myself a few tugs, watching as she glistens with cum from my continuous edging and her eyes shining with lust.

Ignoring her outburst, I brace my weight with one arm next to her head while I use my free hand to guide myself into her heat. Her sharp inhale, high pitched cry, and her tightness squeezing my cock are all signs that she is in for the long haul. Pulling all the way out, I nudge myself back into her until I get further in. Over and over, I work myself inside her and give her a few moments to adjust.

Once I'm nearly all the way in, I retract entirely and slam home.

"Shit!" She screams, her hand flying up to grab my shoulder and dig her nails back into me. It's minimal pain, but it's enough to keep me grounded and aware that she is in no shape to be rough with.

I pause, waiting for her to look up at me. When she does, she is about ready to scream until she sees my face, which immediately softens.

"I hope you know how much I love you, baby," I say sincerely, leaning down to plant my lips on hers. She nods against me and rolls her hips to try and get me to move. I don't comply with her, instead raising backup to look at her face. "I'm serious. You questioned me when I had never given you a reason to. I have been waiting years for you to give me a chance. Why would I ruin that now that you have finally given me a chance? Why would you run instead of talking to me??"

"Not right now," she groans. Her eyes close and head turns to avoid me, probably her attempt to also avoid the question.

"Yes, right now." I rock back into her a few times to get her to loosen up, which works greatly. "If something happened to you...I don't know what I would have done."

"You would have moved on," she huffs as though it's the easiest thing in the world.

"Is that what you would have done?" I retort back and the realization sinks in. "No, you would not have. Let's try this again, and this time, I want you to take this fucking seriously."

Jerking roughly, I slam into her over and over again as she tries to hang on. I fuck her roughly, which is contrary to my previous thoughts, but if she is willing to sass me, I'm willing to fuck the attitude out of her.

"Yes!" She grins as she bounces on my cock. Her legs loop around my hips to lock me in, which doesn't usually work, but I let her guide my thrusts for a few more moments. My balls draw tightly, my spine starts to tingle, and I immediately stop to pull out.

"You could have died!" I shout, realizing that my emotions are suddenly overwhelming me. "They could have fucking taken you to God knows where, and then what? If it weren't for the girls, I never would have known you were pregnant!"

My head whips to the left, my body stiffening in shock from her smacking my cheek.

"If you answered your fucking phone, maybe I could have told you," she grits, shoving my upper body. I don't move. I don't say anything. Instead, I pick up speed and wait until she is coming on my cock before getting up, zipping up my jeans and heading toward the door.

"You have no fucking clue what I am doing for you right now, Birdie. I fucked up, I get that, but *you* left. I didn't fuck that girl, you can ask any of the people at the bar that I shoved her off of me. But no, *you ran.*" She has the audacity to look ashamed of it. "I get you're angry and want to forget what happened, but when you can talk with me like a grown adult instead of taking it out on others, then we can discuss it. Right now, I'm going to let you have some air because I think that's best." Turning on my heel, I touch the door knob before she stops me.

"You don't get to fucking walk away," she calls, her voice wobbly and wet.

"I'm the Devil, and you're my sweetheart. There is no me without you, so I'm not walking away, but I am giving you space. I get that I mean so little to you, but you mean the absolute world to me. I will be back when they do an exam on the baby." With that, I open the door and hurry out of there before I can second guess my decision.

Chapter Eight

BIRDIE

"Wait!" I call out, ripping the blanket off of me and sitting up. The world spins, and before I can fully get out of the bed, several nurses swarm the room.

"You need to lay down, Ms. Yarrow," one in the pink scrubs nicely demands.

"No, I can't," I struggle against their arms, tears welling in my eyes at the thought of Scout leaving me. What have I done? "Please!" I scream, thrashing against their arms to try and get out.

"If you don't calm down, we will sedate you!" The older male nurse yells, and my movements pause. "You need to lay down and get some rest. I don't know what happened, but he will be back," he says in a stern, no bullshit tone. Whipping my head to look up at him, he levels me with a glare. He gives off fatherly vibes. I haven't felt that in a long time, not since my father left. Swallowing thickly, I nod slowly before letting them slide me back into the bed.

□"How do you know?" I croak, terror and a sadening ache settling in my chest. "You don't even know him, how can you even reassure me he will be back?"

□"I will call for a psych consult, Rich," the young female nurse says as she gets ready to walk out.

□"No," the older male nurse, Rich, calls, stopping her in her tracks. "Assign me here for now. Tell the doc that I will be here until the next rotation." I don't know if the man is some big wig, but the girl leaves without even a backwards glance. The rest of the staff file out one by one, making sure that the guy staying behind has whatever he needs.

□He grabs a chair and sidles up next to the bed. Posture relaxed and hands folded on his lap, he doesn't say anything. We stare at one another awkwardly as we both wait for the other to do something. Say something. Maybe he's waiting for me? Fuck, I don't know. After what feels like an hour, he releases a small puff of air before opening his mouth.

□"You asked how I could possibly know what it's like to be in love," he starts. I open my mouth to correct him, but he anticipates this because he puts his hand up in the universal 'stop' motion. "If you're foolish enough to push someone away, then you are in love. It may be platonic or not, but you love them. That's all that matters, Birdie."

"I wouldn't blame him if he didn't come back," I scoff as more tears leak down my cheeks. I swipe them away aggressively, irritated by my own stupidity.

"He will." His stare goes off in the distance for a moment, a wistful look on his face before he turns back to me. "When I saw you, it was like a sense of *deja vu*. Looking in a mirror for my own Clareise. I walked away when I shouldn't have, and I knew from the moment I left that I would never be able to live without her."

He doesn't say anything after that, again looking in the distance for several long moments. The silence grows far too thick for me. "What happened?" My question is barely a whisper in the air, but I know he heard it from the slight twitch in his shoulders.

"We were newer in our relationship, and my father tried to marry me off to another woman. I wanted nothing to do with it, but Clareise wasn't one of those women who took no for an answer. Even if it ended up devastating her..." he trails off, his nose scrunching and eyes glassy as I witness his painful recollection. "She knew she was my everything from the moment she asked me on that date. We may not have been established, but the connection was instant. I had no clue that my father was going to do that to me, to us."

He swallows thickly, his throat bobbing as he attempts to clear the obvious lump in his throat. The redness in his face deepens. "Look man, we don't have to talk about this." I absolutely want to know his story, to get reassurance that Scout might come back...

□"She got so mad," he chokes, smiling sadly at me. "He told me about the supposed engagement the day I told him I wanted to marry Clareise. I swear he had a conniption fit. I remember us both getting into a screaming match about his forcing me to bend to his will. I thought I lost the argument, and *I* wanted to tell Clareise of my father's betrayal. Though I didn't expect her to be happy about it, she was furious. She lashed out at me, which I later realized was self-defense. She told me that she hated me, that she never truly loved me. That she was better off without me...I didn't believe a lick of it, yet I had nothing else to go off of. I thought our futures together had come to an end..."

□"What happened?" I'm metaphorically sitting at the edge of my seat. The fear that I ran Scout out of my life for good has me nearly ready to combust.

□"I married the other woman." A sob escapes my throat at the painful words. He looks pained and angry mixed together, my heart just sad for the man who lost the one thing that meant the most to him. "We married and moved away. I thought about Clareise everyday for the first three months of my marriage. I don't know if it was a miracle of some higher power or what, but the other woman passed away in her sleep when I was away on a trip for my father. When I found out, they immediately questioned me because I couldn't have been more happy. Yes, there was a moment of devastation that a woman had lost her life, but she was the one thing standing between Clareise and I." That's definitely not the outcome I was hoping for. Fuck!

□"I called her the next day, but of course, she wasn't home and no one had her new location, so I flew to her. I knocked on her door incessantly until she answered. She saw my face, slapped me so hard I thought I was going to black out, then kissed me like we wouldn't get another chance."

□"I don't know if I can do that..." I sob, bringing my good hand to cover my mouth. "I can't watch him with another woman. I don't know how I would even function."

□"Then why push him away?" He asks softly. I shake my head, sincerely unsure as to why I do anything at this point. There's no real reason why I pushed him away besides my own feeling of not being good enough. *I know I'm not enough*. "You didn't trust him to talk to him, which caused you to end up here. Tell me about it."

□"I just hate the constant thoughts of never being good enough..." I whimper and sniffle. "He's done so much in making sure that I'm okay, that I'm cared for...when I saw that, I figured he finally decided that I'm not worth the hassle."

"Who told you that you're the hassle?" He counters, his brow poised in question.

"Well, no one, but I *feel* it. The shit I have gone through, Scout picking up every single piece of me that's been shredded and gluing them back together…"

"Birdie," Rich *tsks* almost fatherly and my head snaps straight to look at him. "You're more than worth it. That man," he pauses and points to the door, "is more dedicated than you give him credit for. He's been at your side since the moment we gave him permission. When we weren't sure what your status was, he called the doctor's directly to get the update. He wasn't afraid to get kicked out or called out because he wasn't worried about them. He was worried about *you*. I know you're hurting, but put yourself in his shoes for a moment. Think about what he endured when he got the call that you might be dead? Saw the car upside down and partially crushed knowing that you were inside? The threat on your life? The threat on your unborn baby's life?"

More tears leak from my cheeks and I immediately blame them on the hormones from the baby. Reaching down to touch my stomach, I cradle the non-existent bump.

"How do I make this up to him?" I whisper with need. If there's anything I can accomplish in this lifetime, it will be to ensure that Scout knows just how much I trust him and how sorry I am.

He tilts his head to the side as if it's the most obvious thing in the world. Once he realizes that I have no idea what he's trying to imply, he sighs softly. "You need to show him you love him." He looks like he wants to say more, but he's cut off by a loud knock on the door followed by Sofia and Vivanna barging into the room. He nods at them, waiting until I catch his gaze. I immediately decipher the look as fatherly disappointment, and it doesn't take a rocket scientist to realize I need to get my act together.

"We're so glad you're okay!" Sofia says, walking around Rich to give me a hug.

"Sof and I thought you were dead," Viv cries out while she wipes her nose with a tissue. I chuckle at their overdramatics but realize that they are right. That just makes my situation of pushing Scout away even worse.

I could have died.

I know Scout made that perfectly clear, as did Rich. Yet, for some reason it's just now sinking in that I may not be here right now had Scout not found me. The girls chatter at me about their fears, their conversations with their spouses, and they go into what has happened while I have been cooped up in the hospital.

All I can think about is how I hurt Scout, and what the best way to fix it would be. Since I'm being completely honest with myself, I have no clue how I'm going to make this better. All I know is that I have to. End of story.

Chapter Nine

SCOUT

My fist lands on the punching bag as the whole thing heaves away from me. "Fuck!" I roar as another jab pushes it away. Heavy metal blasts through the speakers as I take my aggression out on this hanging sandbag. No matter how many times I try to relieve the pent up tension inside of me, it's like another wave of agony decides to take over instead.

"Scout," Massimo shouts over the music, tapping on my phone to pause the music. Rolling my eyes I walk over to the bench and unwrap my hands a bit. My shirt lays on the bench where I discarded it earlier, and I use that to wipe the sweat as it drips into my eyes. "Where the fuck have you been?" He barks as he swaggers closer to me. I narrow my eyes at him, my own irritation blooming in my chest.

□"What the fuck do you mean?" I retort, spanning my arms around to motion where I have been all afternoon. It's not like I had anywhere else to be.

□"You were supposed to meet me at the vineyard, dumbass," he scoffs. He shrugs his suit jacket off and comes over to where the gauze and tape are. I eye him cautiously. He barged in here, barked orders at me like I'm his fucking puppy, and now he's wrapping his hands. "We will do this your way. If I win, you will get your ass to the fucking vineyard with me. If you win, you will haul ass back to the hospital and talk to Birdie like a grown ass man."

□"She's the one who fucking pushed me away, man. What more do you want from me? She wanted to fuck, that's what I did. I wanted to figure out what exactly was going through her thick skull when she thought she could run out on me instead of talking with me." The more I talk about it, the more my anger escalates. She can make her own grown up decisions, I get that. What I don't understand is her lack of thinking that shit through. "She not only gave me a reason to walk away, she shoved me out of the fucking door. If she would have fucking talked to me, we wouldn't be here right now."

□"Maybe," he pauses, jerking his head from left to right with a resounding *crack*. "But that doesn't divest from the fact that she is suffering and you showed her that it's easy for you to walk out. Whether or not that is true, actions will always speak louder than words. She was shown a photo of you kissing another woman."

"That was staged," I grit out.

He holds his hands up in a hold on motion. "In any case, actions speak louder. Then when you do show up, you fuck her, display your anger, and leave her there by herself. If it was me and I was in your shoes, there wouldn't be a single soul or deity that could keep me from that room. There will be a time to discuss why she left but this isn't that time. You are a dumbass and don't deserve her if you think otherwise."

□"You know what, fuck you and this fucking game you're playing." I throw my hands up in the air with final defeat, stalking toward the door with my shirt in tow. "We're both hurting right now, yet I need fucking space. She wanted that when she ran away, and now I'm honoring it. God for-fucking-bid I do what she wants!" I shout. I don't realize until I'm mid punch and slam my knuckles into the metal door. Anticipating a throb, I shake out my hand. When it doesn't come, I smirk with glee. Maybe this is the relief I need right now. Rearing back, I do it again and again until two hands grip my elbows and throw me backward. I swear I fly for a moment until I crash land on the boxing mat. The fall knocks the wind out of me and stops me from being able to stand back up right away.

"I get you're pissed off, I really do. But here's the thing," he walks toward me with zero hesitance, grabbing me by the arms to hoist me back to my feet. "You've had time to process your shit. She hasn't. It went from one extreme to the next, then she was out for however long she was. Then whatever shit hit the fan today surely didn't seem to help either one of you. Don't get my shit twisted and think I'm letting her off the hook. What she did was fucked up. She could have died. If that were me, I would have had Sofia's neck on a platter, but that's not me. It's you and your girl. She's got some fucked up trauma, I can see that shit clear as day everytime I talk to her. Give her a bit of grace, man."

Shaking my shoulders out, I seem to deflate. "What did you want to talk about? I swear I didn't know we were meeting today."

"I figured as much. You never seem to miss meetings or anything, so I knew it had to be bad." I nod to confirm everything he said. I don't have the mental capacity for anything else right now, but here I am. Thinking about how I'm going to convince Birdie I'm fucking serious about her staying in my life. "It was actually about the dude who wanted to kill her. Eye for an eye from what it seems like. Though, we were able to trace some other shit back to him..." he paces off, his brows dipping enough that I can see his silent distress. If you didn't know him, you might think he was just being weird and mysterious.

Instead, that's the look of thinking. Usually the topics that draw his brows down aren't good ones.

□Edging closer to him, I prod, "I don't know what you're trying to get at, man." He nods silently, swallowing thickly. "Why would he go after Birdie? That all seems to be based around Sofia?"

□"He was connected with the mafia who took Sofia hostage a few years back." Well that's definitely not what I thought he was going to say. "We had to track her all the way to fucking Alaska. I thought we got them all, but this is clear evidence that we didn't. He told you that you kissed his beloved, or whatever. When he took Sofia, it was for a similar reason. Different, but the principle is the same. I think it makes sense…"

□"So, what are we going to do?" I ask, flopping down onto the bench next to the arena. He sits next to me, his phone in his hands as he scrolls through texts quickly.

□"*I* am going to figure out how to get rid of these fuckers for good. *You* are going to confront Birdie and get your shit together." Scoffing, I drag a single hand through my hair in disbelief. He smacks my arm away from my face and grabs my shoulders harshly. "I'm fucking serious, man. Do I need to fucking beat the shit out of you to get it through your thick skull? This guy," he points to the photo of the dead guy on his device, "was one of the men that almost killed my wife. You think I'm going to advocate for you to have space from your woman? Absolutely not. No one is guaranteed the next minute, yet you're sitting here like you're both going to live forever with enough time to sort through your shit."

"I just need a clear head. Can you fault me for that?" I snap, my mood shifting back to angry within seconds. "I just want to fucking think for a minute and figure out what the fuck I'm doing. I have known her since we were toddlers. She finally gave me a chance then decided that I'm not trustworthy enough. It's bad enough that she couldn't even tell me why she thought that of me. She just fucking *did*. I get she's got trauma, but we all do. We're all some sort of fucked up, and I can't walk around with eggshells for the rest of my life. That will be miserable for both of us. I'm just trying to figure out how I'm going to prove to her that she's the only person I want to do life with." I deflate at the end of my rant. There's no more room for me to bitch and moan at this point. My mental capacity has reached its limit, and I don't know how many times I have to repeat that *I don't want to be away from her*. She pushed me away, and I walked away because if I didn't I know some other shit would have hit the fan.

He doesn't refute my claims, instead scrolling through his phone angrily. I stare over his shoulder and watch as he barely takes a second glance at the shit on his feeds. Finally, after mindless staring for several minutes, an ad pops up on his screen and it's like the world has opened up for me.

I know exactly what I'm going to do.

Chapter Ten

ONE WEEK LATER

BIRDIE

I'm finally getting released from this fucking hell hole. The food is nasty, the showers are cold, and some of the staff are just plain rude. I know I can be cranky, but fucking hell, I didn't realize I needed to *ask* for lunch. Either way, Scout is supposed to be here any minute. My stomach turns at the thought of seeing him again after seven long days. After our fight, he didn't come back. He let me know that he just wanted space and asked that I respect that. I immediately agreed because that shows that I'm more willing to trust him. Trust that he will come back, too.

The first day without him was hell. I didn't think it would hurt so much, but I cried for hours. I ended up running out of tears and dehydrating myself because of it. That night, he texted me. It was simple but effective.

Scout:

> Thank you for the space.

> I love you.

I didn't need to see anything else from him to know that we were going to be okay. Deep inside my gut, I just knew. That, and the morning sickness continued to haunt me and let me know that Scout will be latched onto the two of us for at least eighteen years.

The second day was dreary still, but Rich had visited me again and played board games until he got in trouble. There was only so much I could do since I was confined in my room for direct monitoring, so leaving wasn't an option. Just as I thought I was going to go bat-shit crazy, a delivery came for me. It didn't have a name for who it was from, just an Amazon box with my name. Once I opened it, I immediately knew it was from Scout. Inside there was an adult coloring book with colored pencils, a new series that I wanted to read but never seemed to have the time to read, and also a small teddy bear with a note that said "squish me". When I did, Scout's voice was like a melody through the room.

"Baby bird, I know we're both having a hard time, but I wanted you to hear this from me. I need you more than I need air to breathe. You're my world, and I just wanted you

to hear that from me. I will be there when they discharge you, don't fret, baby bird."

In case there was confusion, I sobbed like a baby again after hearing that. I'm blaming it on the hormones, but we all know that it was because he professed his love again. Any woman would swoon for that.

On the third day, I sat and stared at the wall until the nursing staff directed me around. They helped me bath, change, then get back into bed to eat all three meals when they actually came. I also kept the blinds closed because there wasn't any point in seeing the sun rise and fall. It was painful to watch the days continue to shine brightly while I felt so glum. So, they stayed closed. After that, the days all seemed to blur together. Sofia and Viv visited me every day, bringing me things to do while I waited to be discharged. Massimo even stopped by one of those days with Sofia and gave me flowers. It was odd, because I can't recall a time where I had ever been given flowers from anyone other than Scout. Thinking even harder about it, I think he only got me flowers a handful of times.

Now, the last day is here, and that's where all my subdued excitement has come into play. He may not have outright promised that he would be here, but Scout is a man of his word. I have faith that he will come through for me, even if we're arguing or fighting.

A knock lands heavily on the door as a brunette girl cracks the door open. "Hi, I'm Lacy from billing, can I come in?" She asks. I nod, motioning for her to enter. "So, I was just going through your paperwork and noticed that you don't have any insurance. It's not a big deal, but we wanted to be able to double check that with you or figure out your potential payment plans."

"Uhm," I stutter, unsure what she's talking about. "Payment plans for what? I know health care isn't free, but I thought you all would just bill me?" I ask incredulously. I can't remember a time where I stayed in the hospital and had to worry about it. Scout was usually always by my side.

"I got it," the deep, baritone voice that I fell in love with says. We both look toward him, and I swear this bitch has hearts in her eyes. "Birdie will be billed under my insurance." He enters the room fully with a trail of people. Massimo, Sofia, Vivianna and a few of Scout's other friends enter the room.

"Scout, I can't just be added to your insurance," I laugh nervously, tucking a strand of hair behind my ear.

What has gotten into this man? First he leaves me for a week and now he is talking about adding me to his insurance?

"You can be added if you are my wife." The words tumble from his mouth so nonchalantly that I almost don't catch them. "We can either get married here and now, at the courthouse down the road, or we can wait until after the baby is born. If I had my choice, I would say we do it at the courthouse, but it's totally up to you.

Regardless, you are going to be my wife and that is not up for discussion. Choose now, baby bird, so the preparations can begin with whichever path you choose."

My ears start ringing, my eyes well up with tears, and I swear I pass out because when I blink, Scout is down on one knee by the bed. His hand cradles mine as he brings a ring to my finger. My nose burns as tears cloud my vision.

□"Birdie, I didn't know how else to prove to you that you are my everything. This was the only way I could think of that was a grand enough gesture that would get it through your thick skull." A watery giggle escapes me as he brings my knuckles up to his lips for a gentle kiss. "Baby Bird, you are the moon in the sky, forever with me in the light of the day and in the darkest of nights. I have always wanted to be the one impulse that you never denied yourself. I want to be the raft you hold on to in the roughest of waters, the lighthouse that guides you home. I want to be the one that roars louder than your demons and feeds your primal desires. I will assimilate your trauma and return it to you as love, passion, and understanding. I have waited a lifetime for this chance to love you without hesitation and I would choose you in every lifetime, in every world, and every version of reality. I would always find you, my moon, for you always pull me towards you. Birdie Yarrow, will you please accept my love and commitment by marrying me?"

I nod like a crazy person, tears pouring from my face and onto our joined hands. Of all rings I've seen, this has to be the most unique, which brings fresh tears to the surface. The moon wraps around a stone that looks like the starry sky on a cloudless night. There are stars that climb each side of the band and I see all the physical representations of our love in this ring. When it's settled onto my finger in its rightful place, he kisses me like there is no tomorrow.

As the room fades away, there is no one but him. Thinking back, I can't help but feel that there was a time where I may not have been there for him at all. For a while there, I thought it was all going to end, and I didn't see a way back for us. I thought that my life was over when Scout walked out that door and didn't come back. Without him in my life, there was no purpose. I had no reason to look forward to the day, no reason to pull myself out of the hole I was in. I never truly realized till he was gone, just how much Scout was integrated into every aspect of my life. Hearing him say those words, professing his love to me, and bringing our friends as witnesses, solidified for me that he is my sun as I am his moon. My heart feels full to the highest extent knowing that he feels exactly the same as I do.

"So, are we going to the courthouse or does Massimo have to marry us?" His face is so serious, and I can't help the laugh I let out from this insanity.

"Courthouse."

"Viv and I took the liberty of grabbing a few for you to try. We didn't have a lot of choices to begin with, so we're sorry about that." These damn pregnancy hormones have taken over because more tears well in my eyes. I would have never anticipated someone doing these things for me, but here we are.

□"Please don't cry, I need to do your makeup and wet skin isn't it," Viv reprimands gently. I nod, sniffling and trying to get myself to chill the fuck out. The rag dries my cheeks and is poised under my eyes while I blink out the last of them.

□"Alright, I'm done. Don't talk about soft stuff right now, my hormones can't take it," I retort with sarcasm leaking off my tone. Though, I'm definitely not joking. If they keep that shit up, I'll keep sobbing.

□They pull one of the dresses from the garment bag and I can immediately rule it out.□

Once the second dress comes out of the bag, I know I'm sold. The dress shimmers in the sunlight from the room, glistening like a halo on it. There is a corset made from organza and shiny tulle with voluminous sleeves that seem to start mid-bicep. There are crystals, beads, and sequins scattered along the dress in the most perfect patterns of stars. The skirt is longer than the dress itself, which means it's a train to flow behind.

◻"That's the one."

"You look stunning, Birdie," Viv coos with a sniffle. I roll my eyes at the outward affection, but the emotions behind her words have me gasping for air in the best possible way. Turning around slowly to face the mirror, I am blown away by what they were able to accomplish in such a short time and little preparation. I don't recognize myself.

A knock brings me out of the stare off with myself, and Massimo peeks his head into the room. "If you ladies don't hurry up, I believe Scout will barge in here and drag her to the altar," he says very seriously. There's a very slight glimmer in his eyes that gives me the slightest indication that he's being sarcastic.

Breathing several times, I decide to just walk. I don't wait for the girls to follow me, instead rolling my shoulders back as best I can and walking to the main room.

He's standing with Massimo and the Officiant. He doesn't see me yet as his back is turned and facing away. I see them patting his back and reassuring him quietly as I get closer and closer.. I can see the tissue he is dabbing his eyes with. Sophia wraps her arm around mine as we breach the doorway. As my foot comes over the frame, Massimo taps Scout on the shoulder.

I wait on bated breath for him to turn around. It's almost slow motion, and the butterflies are taking flight in my stomach. The moment our eyes connect, I watch the literal firework explosion in his. He sucks in a sharp breath, bringing his fist to his mouth, and his eyes begin to descend my body to the dress I chose. I am watching him closely and cataloging this moment for my memory. His tears begin to flow down his cheeks as my own eyes well up in tears.

This may not have been the wedding I would have chosen but marrying him is the best decision I will make. Forever my northern star.

Crisis Hotlines

I f you or someone you love are in need of emergency assistance, do not hesitate to call your local emergency number. Professionals are there to assist you as needed. All hotlines are FREE.

National Sexual Assault Hotline/Support Lines:
Australia: 1800 737 723
Canada: 604-255-6344
Germany: 08000116016
USA: 1-800-656-4673 or 877-995–5247
UK: 0808 500 2222

Suicide and Crisis Hotlines:
Australia: 13 11 14
Canada: 519-416-486-2242
Germany: 0800-181-0721
UK: 08457-90-90-90
USA: (800) 723-8255 or Dial 988

Crisis Textline:

Canada: Text HOME to 686868 for Self-Harm Help

USA: Text CONNECT to 741741 for Self-Harm Help

UK: Text SHOUT to 85258 for Self-Harm Help

About the

Author

Lexi Gray is an Alaskan-Based author with several years of freelance editing under her belt. Ms. Gray has also dabbled in narrating, which can be found on Audible. She's had a passion for writing at an early age; however, started out in helping authors develop their writing skills and bringing languid movement and passion to their works. Her unique voice shines through her works, using emotion-based writing and hitting subjects that may present as taboo. Ms. Gray utilizes critical thinking and good, dirty and dark humor to get through it all.

Her hope is that when readers pick up her works, or the works of others she's helped along the way, they'll be stuck with their nose in it.

Ms. Gray herself enjoys reading dark romance, but also loves to dive into a dirty RomCom or two. From her own past experiences, she hopes to use her books as a sense of learning for those who read it, even if they end up only holding it with one hand along the way...IYKYK.

You can check out updates along the way on her Instagram:

@AuthorLexiGray or on her website at AuthorLexiGray.com

Also By

Satan on Wheels by Lexi Gray is a slow-burn, enemies to loves, motorcycle club thriller that you don't want to miss! Action packed full of fan-favorite tropes and triggers! Don't forget, smut starts on page one! It's book one of the Rubber Down Duology.

Satan's Naughty List is book two of the Rubber Down Duology. Another action packed motorcycle club story, featuring your favorite duo from book one! This is an RH, MM/MMF love story. HEA guaranteed. Again, smut starts in chapter one!

Action packed Why Choose/Reverse Harem motorcycle club romance! Explore the world of Domme Fatal in this action-packed thriller! HEA guaranteed.

Acknowledgements

Thank you to my amazing husband for supporting my craziness through and through!

To my lovely PA Chardonae Davis for helping me get everything promoted for this amazing new read. She has been a major backbone for me as an author, and I can't express how much I appreciate her. Love you, boo!

To my amazing Alpha & Beta teams as well as the ARC team, y'all help me piece my stories together, and without you, this would be a hell of a lot harder to do!

Lastly, but most importantly, I want to thank **YOU,** reader. Thank you for taking the time to read this piece of my art and sharing it with the world. Thank you for giving this small town author a chance to experience new heights.

Without you, I wouldn't exist.

Made in the USA
Columbia, SC
16 September 2024

42411687R00048